PIGGINS AND THE ROYAL WEDDING

PIGGINS AND THE ROYAL WEDDING

BY JANE YOLEN

ILLUSTRATED BY JANE DYER

HARCOURT BRACE JOVANOVICH, PUBLISHERS

San Diego   New York   London

For Kathy and Joey
and true love

Requests for permission to make copies of any
part of the work should be mailed to:
Permissions, Harcourt Brace Jovanovich, Publishers,
Orlando, Florida 32887.

Library of Congress Cataloging-in-Publication Data
Yolen, Jane.
Piggins and the royal wedding/by Jane Yolen;
illustrated by Jane Dyer.—1st ed.
p.   cm.
Summary: Piggins, the butler at the Reynard
household, solves the mystery of
the missing royal wedding band.
ISBN 0-15-261687-X
[1. Mystery and detective stories.
2. Pigs—Fiction. 3. Animals—Fiction.]
I. Dyer, Jane, ill. II. Title.
PZ7.Y78Pj   1989
[E]—dc19   88-5399

First edition

A B C D E

The illustrations in this book were done in
colored pencil and Luma dyes on
140-lb. Fabriano hot press watercolor paper.

The display type was set in Baskerville and
the text type was set in Baskerville No. 2
by Thompson Type, San Diego, California.

Printed and bound by Tien Wah Press, Singapore

Production supervision by Warren Wallerstein
and Ginger Boyer
Designed by Camilla Filancia
based on a design by Dalia Hartman

Trit-trot, trit-trot. That is the sound of Piggins, the butler at 47 The Meadows, going up the stairs. He is carrying clean gloves for all the Reynards to wear.

UPSTAIRS   Mr. and Mrs. Reynard are dressing in their finest. Diamond buttons for Mr. Reynard. Mrs. Reynard wears a diamond ring.

"You will be the loveliest lady at the royal wedding," Mr. Reynard says gallantly.

"Always excepting the bride," Mrs. Reynard reminds him. "After all, she is my closest friend."

"And always excepting the Queen," Mr. Reynard says, bowing his head.

They smile fondly at one another.

Nanny Bess is dressing the children. They get diamonds, too. A diamond bracelet for Trixy. A diamond stickpin for Rexy. The little ones get glass, for they do not know the difference.

BELOW STAIRS   The servants have the rest of the day off. Dressed in their Sunday best, they are going to stand outside the cathedral and wave their handkerchiefs when the royal bride and groom drive away.

The kitchen is spotless. Cook puts on her bonnet. Jane adjusts her petticoat. Even Sara is neat and clean. That has been the biggest job of all.

IN THE HALL   Piggins sets out the hats and coats. He gives them a careful brushing. Nothing but the very best is good enough for a royal wedding, Piggins knows.

The carriage sent from the palace is waiting outside. Nanny Bess and the littlest kits climb in.

Rexy pats the horse. He is excited because he gets to carry the wedding ring on a big pillow. He is so excited he has not been able to eat all day.

Trixy is excited, too. She is to be one of the flower girls. She has been practicing walking down the aisle for weeks and has worn a little path in the nursery rug.

"Good-bye," Mrs. Reynard calls to the servants. "Be sure to get close enough for a good view."

Mr. Reynard gives Piggins last-minute instructions. Of all the servants, only Piggins will stay at home. He does not like crowds.

The carriage rolls through big streets and narrow streets, through straight streets and winding streets. There are happy onlookers everywhere. They wave handkerchiefs and flags.

In the streets and on the sidewalks are ribbon sellers and flower sellers, flag sellers and sellers of fruit pies. Chocolates and other

candies made in the shape of the King's crown and the bride's ring
are for sale on every street corner. There are organ grinders with
pet monkeys and puppet players who put on shows. Rexy even sees
a pickpocket, but before he can tell his father, the thief has escaped
into the crowd.

At last the carriage arrives at the cathedral. The cathedral is already full. Everyone is sitting down except for the bride and groom and members of the wedding party. They are in the back rooms.

Mr. and Mrs. Reynard take Trixy and Rexy to the back, greeting old friends as they go. They smile at Professor T. Ortoise and wave at Pierre Lapin. They throw kisses at the three unmarried Lapin sisters. They notice Inspector Bayswater keeping an eye on the crowd.

Trixy goes into the left-hand room. There is the bride. She is wearing a white gown sewn with hundreds of tiny pearls. She and the other flower girls give Trixy a hug.

The maid of honor hands Trixy a bouquet of roses and baby's breath, the bride's favorite. When Trixy turns around, she sees the Queen.

"Oh, Your Majesty," says Trixy, dropping an elegant, deep curtsey. She has been practicing that as well.

Rexy goes into the right-hand room. There is the groom in his grey suit. He holds his hat in his hand.

"Here at last, young Reynard," says Lord Molesly, the groom's best man. He hands Rexy a plump pillow.

There is a ring attached to the top of the pillow. It is held on by a single silken thread.

Rexy hugs the pillow tightly. His stomach feels full of butterflies.

Suddenly the King enters the room. Everyone bows low,
especially Rexy. When they straighten up again, the ring is gone!
"The ring!" Rexy cries. "Where is the wedding ring?"
"The royal wedding ring!" says the groom.

"That ring has been in my family for generations," shouts the King. "Who is the thief?"

"The ring bearer," proclaims Lord Molesly. "It must have been Rexy. Who else was nearby?"

They send for Inspector Bayswater, who arrives with three policemen. Rexy is very frightened. He is so frightened he drops the pillow.

The policemen look around the room, behind curtains, under tables, in back of chairs, inside flowerpots. They even check the chandelier. But there is no sign of the ring. The only clues are a slight smudge on the pillow, a long piece of silken thread, and some crumpled silver paper on the floor.

The groom wipes his face with his handkerchief. The king twists a lock of his hair. Lord Molesly frowns at Rexy before ducking his face from the bright light of the electric torches. The groomsmen all turn out their pockets and shake their heads. Mr. Reynard comforts Rexy.

"It is no good, Your Majesty," says Inspector Bayswater. "We can find nothing."

"Why not send for my butler, Piggins?" asks Mr. Reynard. "He is a whiz at solving mysteries."

"Yes, indeed," agrees Inspector Bayswater.

"Anything," says the King. "Only we must find that ring!"

The police wagon is sent to 47 The Meadows, where Piggins is
just settling down for a cup of tea.

Two policemen hurry Piggins into the wagon, and they race
back to the cathedral.

At the cathedral Piggins is led directly into the back room.

"What is the matter?" he asks.

Rexy is crying. "They say I stole the royal wedding ring."

"Stuff and nonsense," says Mr. Reynard. "Piggins will set it all straight." He pats Rexy on the head.

Inspector Bayswater explains. He shows Piggins the pillow with

its smudge. He shows Piggins the thread. He shows Piggins the crumpled silver paper. Then he shows Piggins all the places the police have looked for the ring.

"The ring bearer *must* have taken it and hidden it," says Lord Molesly. "No one else had a chance."

Piggins thinks a moment. "That," he says, "is not strictly true."

Piggins takes the silver paper and smoothes it out. He sniffs it and smiles. Then he looks carefully at the pillow and sniffs it as well.

"Just as I thought," he says. "Inspector, what do you think?"

Bayswater sniffs both paper and pillow himself. "Why," he says, surprised, "chocolate. And marzipan. And a touch of mint."

"Exactly," says Piggins. "The ring young Rexy was handed atop that pillow was not an old family heirloom at all. It was a clever fake made of candy and wrapped in silver paper. When the King came in, everyone bowed as the thief knew they would. At that very moment, the thief yanked on an all-but-invisible thread tied to the ring. The fake ring was pulled from the pillow, leaving a faint chocolate smudge. In the confusion that followed, the thief stripped off the silver paper and popped the candy into his mouth, thus disposing of the evidence."

"But where is the real ring?" asks the King.

"In the real thief's home," says Piggins.

"And who is the real thief?" asks the groom.

"Just check everyone's gloves," says Piggins. "For chocolate stains."

The police check the gloves. Rexy has a stain on his left glove, but it smells like horse. One of the groomsmen has a definite chocolate smudge between his thumb and forefinger. The police lead him away.

Though it is a little late getting started, the wedding goes on as planned. Mrs. Reynard lends the bride her diamond ring. It fits perfectly.

"Did the groomsman do it for love?" Mrs. Reynard whispers to her husband.

He shakes his head. "No, he did it for the money, my dear."

"How unromantic," she says with a sigh.

"Not at all like you," he answers.

They smile at one another fondly.

Rexy and Trixy make no mistakes. They walk up the aisle smiling broadly. When they get near the back of the cathedral, there is Piggins. Trixy takes one of the roses and gives it to him.

"Thank you, Piggins," she says. "Thank you for saving my favorite brother."

"Your *only* brother," mumbles Rexy. But he is pleased.

The bride and groom climb into the royal wedding coach and drive away.

Everyone in the crowd waves a handkerchief. Cook and Jane are near the gate. Sara is nowhere in sight.

UPSTAIRS   Nanny Bess helps Trixy with her nightgown. Rexy and the little kits are already fast asleep. It has been a long, tiring day.

BELOW STAIRS   Cook and Jane talk about the bride and groom over a cup of tea.

"She was so beautiful," says Cook.

"He was so handsome," says Jane.

They sigh.

Sara comes in the door. She is dirty and bedraggled.

"Where were you?" they ask. "What happened?"

"I got lost," Sara says. "And somebody stole my pocketbook."

"What was in it?" Cook asks.

Sara sighs. "Only my handkerchief. And four chocolates," she says. "But they looked just like the royal wedding ring. I had one for each of us."

IN THE LIVING ROOM   Mr. and Mrs. Reynard thank Piggins. Mr. Reynard gives him a medal, one of his very own. Mrs. Reynard gives him a kiss on the cheek.

"Our Piggins," they say.

Piggins actually blushes.

As he goes down the stairs, Piggins looks at the medal. It says *First Honors*. He smiles. He knows there are lots of gloves to clean, but he decides to wait and do them in the morning. *Trit-trot. Trit-trot. Trit-trot.*